HORSELAND

Horseland #4: Rein or Shine
Copyright © 2008 DIC Entertainment Corp.
Horseland property ™ Horseland LLC
Printed in the United States of America.
www.harpercollinschildrens.com
www.horseland.com

Library of Congress catalog card number: 2007933981
ISBN 978-0-06-134170-0

Book design by Sean Boggs

First Edition

Rein or Shine

Adapted by
SADIE CHESTERFIELD
Based on the episode
"THE CAN-DO KID"
Written by
MARTHA MORAN

HarperEntertainment
An Imprint of HarperCollins Publishers

CHAPTER 1

In the middle of a beautiful countryside sits Horseland, a sprawling ranch. Riders who come to Horseland find exciting adventures in the surrounding mountains and acres of wild forest, and create great friendships along the way. With a large stable, a tackroom, and—best of all—an arena for training, Horseland is the greatest place around to board, groom, and show a horse.

Shep, an Australian shepherd herding dog,

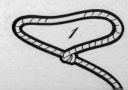

stands in Horseland's arena. Shep is in charge of the stables at Horseland, and is known to rule with an iron paw. He watches Will Taggert, the nephew of Horseland's owners, swirl a lasso over his head. Across from Will stands a wooden post with horns nailed to it, a perfect target for lassoing. Will tosses the lasso, but the loop just misses the post.

"I've got to hand it to Will. He sure is persistent," Shep says, nodding his head in approval. Angora, the beautiful gray cat who is always lounging around the farm—this time on a bale of hay—rolls over and opens one of her green eyes.

"I'd wish he'd stop," she says sleepily. "He's ruining my nap." Shep watches as Will tosses the lasso again and again. He misses his target every time, but he doesn't get frustrated. He just keeps practicing.

"He'll get it, sooner or later," Shep says in his soft, reassuring voice, "just got to keep trying." Teeny, the spotted potbellied pig, stands on another nearby bale of hay and

watches as Will throws the lasso high into the air. "It's up, it's flying, it's, it's—" but before Teeny can say another word the lasso flies out of Will's hands and around Angora, who lets out an annoyed *meow*.

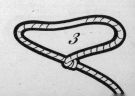

3

"Yup," Shep says with a smile. "It's going to take a lot of perseverance and patience."

Shep is right. He's learned firsthand what perseverance can do . . . from Sarah and Scarlet.

CHAPTER 2

After days and days of rain, the skies above Horseland had finally cleared. No one was happier than the horses. They had been cooped up in their stalls for the last week while the rain pummeled the stable. But today, in the nice weather, everyone was back outdoors.

A beautiful black horse bolted out of the stables and splashed through the mud puddles in the open field. A brown horse with a white mane trotted close behind.

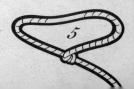

"Finally, some sun!" Molly cried. Molly Washington trotted along on Calypso, her brown-spotted Appaloosa. It felt good to be outside again, in the cool fresh air.

"Woohoo!" Molly shouted, as Calypso broke off into a fast gallop. They sprayed a puddle of water over Angora, who was taking a stroll around the stable.

Some days it just doesn't pay to get out of bed, she thought, shaking the water from her fur.

Alma Rodriguez and her skewbald pinto mare named Button followed Calypso and Molly down toward the stables. The other riders were still gathering their gear.

"Come on, let's get a move on!" Molly shouted excitedly to Sarah Whitney. Sarah was trim and blond and was combing the mane of her Arabian mare Scarlet. When she finished, she pulled on her red riding jacket.

"Before it starts raining again," Alma added, pulling Button up alongside Sarah. But a ride was the last thing on Sarah's mind. She pulled out four sheets of paper

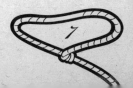

and handed one to each of the other girls. The redheaded Stilton sisters, Chloe and Zoey, scrunched their noses in disapproval.

"Oh, no! Not more dressage moves!" Zoey said uneasily. Alma studied her sheet and frowned.

"This looks complicated," she said.

Chloe glanced at the page, which showed a horse walking sideways, one hoof crossing over the other. She read out the directions.

"Foreleg yield to the left. Squeeze firmly with your right leg on or slightly behind the girth. Use contact with the outside rein to control the forward movement. So the horse's feet are going *this* way," Chloe said, stepping out to the right, "and we're going *that* way and—I don't know, Chili. What do you think about this?" she said, giggling. The gray Dutch Warmblood stallion responded by gently nudging his rider and knocking her over!

"You know what they say. . . ." Molly said as everyone, including Chloe, laughed.

"Yeah," Sarah replied. "Take it one hoof

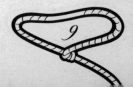

at a time—which I intend to do, just as soon as we get back from our ride." Sarah lifted the heavy saddle onto Scarlet's back.

Alma glanced sideways at Molly. Sarah was always so eager to master new steps and to challenge Scarlet, but she sometimes got carried away. "Miss Overachiever rides again," Alma kidded.

"It's okay, Sarah," Molly offered. "You don't have to learn it all in one day."

Sarah grinned and patted Scarlet's flank. "I think Scarlet can handle it," she said confidently.

Just then, Zoey and Chloe started shrieking and hopping around excitedly, their hands flailing in the air. "Mouse! Mouse!" they screamed, as a tiny gray field mouse darted around their riding boots. Zoey tried to jump up onto Pepper, her gray Dutch Warmblood mare, but her saddle wasn't fastened. She flew over the horse and back onto some feed bags in the corner of the stable. More mice ran out from beneath her.

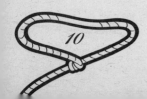

Nearby, Shep and Teeny were watching the commotion. Shep shook his head and headed off for the greenhouse. He was in charge of the stables, but he was going to need some serious feline assistance to solve this problem. Where was that lazy cat?

Shep stood in the doorway of the greenhouse. "Angora! I know you're in there. You're needed *now*!" he called out. Inside, Angora lounged on an old velvet pillow. She turned her head to look at Shep and stretched out her legs.

"Why do dogs always need a cat to take care of business?" she asked. Shep rolled his eyes and turned back toward the stables.

"This is your line of work, not mine," he said, as Angora followed wearily behind him, still half asleep.

At the stables, a few mice ran this way and that. Some darted through the horses' stalls. Angora took one look at them and

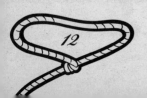

started howling. This was disgusting!

"Sorry," she said, "just not interested."

"I thought cats *loved* to chase mice," Teeny said, confused.

"It's too much work. I need my catnap." With her tail held high, Angora stalked off.

Shep let out a sigh. It was useless. He had lived at Horseland long enough to know— Angora was no ordinary cat.

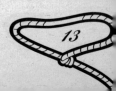

CHAPTER 3

Molly, Alma, and Sarah raced through the field and into the arena gate. They had just gone on the most amazing ride with their horses, up through the wilderness trails behind Horseland. Sarah jumped down from Scarlet and patted her on the neck.

"What a nice ride," Molly said with a sigh.

"It was a beautiful day for trail riding," Alma added, looking up at the blue sky.

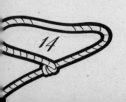

"Time to get started on that dressage move," Sarah said. Molly and Alma groaned.

"But we've been riding hard for hours," Molly said.

"I need a break, *chica*," Alma said. "So does Button."

Sarah looked at Scarlet and smiled. "Scarlet can handle it. Can't you, girl?" she asked. Scarlet let out a tired whinny. "Who's going to join me?" It was no use—once Sarah set her mind on something, it was as good as done.

In the arena, Sarah studied the directions for the dressage move. She squeezed her right leg into Scarlet's side while pulling in on the left rein. "OK girl, let's try going to the left." Scarlet tossed her head, not certain what to do. Sarah patted her side.

"I don't know what I'm doing either. Let's try again," she said encouragingly.

Alma and Molly gave in and led their horses into the arena to practice.

"Half hour max, okay, *bueno*?" Alma

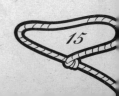

15

assured Button. "Then it's cocoa for me and carrots for you."

Molly smiled. "Make mine with marshmallows!" she said.

Chloe and Zoey rode up outside the arena gate and stood there on their horses, Chili and Pepper. Chloe and Zoey Stilton weren't like the other girls at Horseland—the two sisters were competitive and even a little sneaky. And, worst of all, they were always looking for an opportunity to tease Alma, Molly, and Sarah. Chloe watched as the girls pulled at their reins, trying to get their horses to do the difficult dressage move.

"You girls sure know how to ruin a primo day!" Chloe said, smirking.

"Yeah." Zoey laughed. "*Dull*-sage can wait until tomorrow." They gave the girls one more pitiful look before they trotted away.

Sarah and Scarlet watched Chloe and Zoey ride off. Scarlet would have preferred

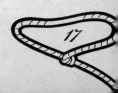

to wait until tomorrow, too, but she didn't want to disappoint Sarah.

"Forget them," Sarah said finally. "We want to nail this, don't we, girl?" Sarah pulled again at the left rein and pressed her right leg into Scarlet's side. But Scarlet didn't move. She still had her eyes locked on Chili and Pepper, their backsides disappearing into the stable. This was going to be a *long* day.

As the sun began to set, Scarlet and Sarah continued practicing. Scarlet moved her legs out to the side, crossed her right hooves over her left, but then fell off balance. She let out a frustrated snort.

Exhausted, Molly and Alma led their horses out of the arena. They turned back to Sarah as they headed for the barn.

"It's time for some cocoa—should I make some for you, *mi amiga*?" Alma asked. But Sarah and Scarlet weren't going anywhere. There was still work to do.

"No, thanks," Sarah said. She rested her hand on Scarlet's black mane and whispered

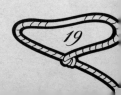

into her ear. "Come on, Scarlet, just a little longer."

Scarlet and Sarah were still practicing hours later. The arena was dark, and there were no other horses around. Scarlet let out a tired whinny as she attempted to step her left leg over her right. Sarah stroked her neck.

"One more try, and then we'll quit, okay?" Sarah said softly. Scarlet gazed longingly at the stable. *Just one more try*—hadn't Sarah said that an hour ago?

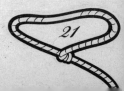

CHAPTER 4

The next morning, Scarlet stood in the stable, exhausted. Sarah had kept her out late, practicing the dressage step over and over and over again. Every muscle in her body hurt. As the sun rose, the horses could hear a truck pulling up outside. Button perked up her ears.

"That sounds like Sarah's car. Isn't it kind of early?" she asked. Button was right. It definitely was Sarah's car. Scarlet let out a weary sigh. Her legs were still sore from last night.

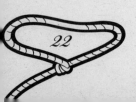

The last thing she wanted to do was more dressage practice.

"She's relentless. You could pretend your legs are sore," Button suggested. Scarlet snorted.

"They *are* sore!" she cried. "I love Sarah's perseverance, but new stuff like this takes time. . . . You have to have patience. You can't just learn it overnight."

The stable door swung open and Sarah stepped inside, beaming. She handed Scarlet a big carrot and stroked her muzzle.

"Hi, girl! I know it's early, but the weatherman says it's going to rain this afternoon." Sarah patted Scarlet's nose and walked to the other side of the stable to get her saddle and gear. Button and Scarlet exchanged a worried look.

As Sarah placed her saddle over Scarlet's back, Alma and Molly entered the barn and spotted Sarah.

"More leg yielding?" Alma asked.

"I know we can get it if we just keep at it," Sarah said confidently. Alma reached into her leather knapsack and pulled out a burgundy book.

"Check this out, Sarah. I got it from the library last night. I kept thinking, dressage is so . . . unnatural. I kept wondering—why would anyone make horses do all those

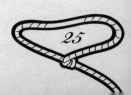

weird moves? But it's actually pretty cool." Alma opened to a page she had marked in the book. On it was an illustrated picture of a medieval battlefield. Two armies were approaching from opposite hillsides, both on horseback. Alma turned the book toward Sarah and launched into an explanation. "It started way back in the Middle Ages when horses were used in battle. A warlord could use a dressage move to make it look like an army was moving when they were really standing still."

"Ha!" Molly laughed. "Like the moon-walk." Alma turned a page. There was another illustration of a horse charging, its rider dodging flying spears. The horse was step-ping high in the air, doing a lateral dressage move.

"It really makes you appreciate the tradi-tion more," Sarah said. Alma nodded and read the caption below the picture.

"The lateral steps were a tactical move for fighting—to make the rider and horse a

smaller target. Cool, huh?" Sarah took the book from Alma's hands and stared at the illustrated pages. It was definitely very cool.

"Don't worry, Button," Alma said softly, turning to the mare. "I'm not planning to take you into battle anytime soon." But Button let out a startled whinny and jerked her head away. She stepped high in the air, pulling her hooves up furiously. Alma looked down and saw . . . more mice! They were running all around her feet!

"Ew!" she screamed, jumping up and down on one foot.

Shep was on guard and watched as several mice darted through the stalls. He let out a low growl. Angora was going to have to scare away these mice, whether she liked it or not.

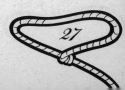

CHAPTER 5

Shep ran out of the stable and through the yard. Teeny was rolling around in the grass. When she saw Shep dart past, she knew something was wrong.

"Hey, Shep, where you going?" she asked. "Can I come? Can I? Can I?"

"More mice," Shep replied. "Need Angora." Teeny followed Shep to the greenhouse, where Angora was fast asleep on a pillow, the sunlight from the window warming

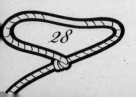

her. They could hear her snores from the doorway. Shep let out a disgusted sigh.

"Do cats do anything but sleep?" he asked. Angora opened her eyes and curled further into herself. When would Shep leave her alone? She needed her beauty rest.

"Do dogs do anything but annoy cats?" she asked, through a sleepy yawn. With that, Angora rolled over and went back to sleep.

That did it. Shep looked around the greenhouse, past the potted tulips and hydrangeas. His eyes rested on the sprinkler system overhead.

"What are you up to, Shep?" Teeny asked, giving him a curious look.

"I'm going to make that cat do what a cat's supposed to do!" Shep said, already hatching a plan. Shep walked out the door and into the afternoon air. Teeny followed close behind. On the wall outside the door, he saw what he was looking for. He pushed his paw hard against a flat white

button, and water blasted from all the sprinkler heads in the greenhouse. Angora was soaked!

Angora let out an annoyed howl. She jumped from her pillow onto the window ledge and darted out the window. She ran around the outside of the greenhouse, care-

ful not to be seen. Shep wasn't going to get away with this.

"Very funny." Angora growled. "But Shep's not the only one who knows how to push buttons."

Shep and Teeny stood outside the doorway, waiting for a sopping wet Angora to emerge, furious. But she never did. Where was she? Shep and Teeny turned off the sprinkler and walked slowly into the greenhouse, past all the daisies and the marigolds, toward Angora's velvet pillow. Teeny gave Shep a puzzled look as they stared at the velvet pillow, which sat alone on a wooden table in the back. Angora had disappeared.

Meanwhile, Angora creeped around the front of the house, where Shep and Teeny had been standing just moments before. Now was her chance! She pressed the flat white button on the wall and the sprinklers blasted water again, this time soaking Shep and Teeny. Shep let out an angry bark as he

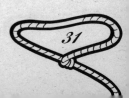

stumbled out of the greenhouse, his fur dripping wet. A puddle spread out beneath his paws. Angora laughed and sashayed past, flicking her long gray tail in Shep's face. That was the last time Shep would bother *this* cat!

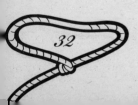

CHAPTER 6

ater that afternoon, the dark clouds returned over Horseland. It looked as though rain would pour any second. In the center of the arena, Sarah pulled left on Scarlet's reins and the horse took a step to the left. They were close to getting the lateral move. If only they had just a few more hours to practice . . .

"Again," Sarah said, shaking her head. But Scarlet was frustrated and tired. They had been at it all afternoon. Scarlet's forelegs

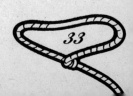

moved cautiously to the right, but suddenly she fell off balance. She had to step left to steady herself. Sarah sighed. Scarlet was so close to getting it—she just had to try a little harder.

"You almost had it, girl!" Sarah said encouragingly. "Let's go again." So Scarlet tried again . . . and again . . . and again. But every time, she fell off balance and couldn't complete the move.

"Again!" Sarah called out. Scarlet let out a tired snort. Slowly, she moved to the right, and this time she got it.

"Again, girl," Sarah said. She knew Scarlet could do it faster. Suddenly, the sound of thunder split the silence of the cool night. Sarah looked up at the dark sky. A heavy drop of rain hit her shoulder and rolled off her jacket. There was little time.

"Come on, girl, six steps in a row and we'll quit."

Molly and Calypso were returning from their trail ride when they spotted Sarah and

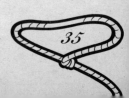

Scarlet in the center of the arena. Molly looked at the sky, nervous, then pulled alongside the fence.

"Sarah, come on!" Molly shouted. "It's about to pour!"

But they were so close! Sarah just needed a few more minutes. "But she's almost got it!" she called to Molly. "I know we can do this!" Scarlet let out an exhausted whinny.

"Poor Scarlet," Molly said softly, shaking her head. Calypso neighed in agreement. Scarlet was hunched over, exhausted.

Suddenly, the sky flashed with lightning. Thunder rumbled. Spooked, Scarlet reared up on her hind legs. She took an awkward step backward, and her hoof rolled sideways, going down hard. Scarlet let out a yelp. Sarah hopped off her quickly and looked at the injured leg, which Scarlet was holding in the air. Scarlet was panting hard as her ankle swelled up.

"Oh no, Scarlet!" Sarah cried, holding tight to the horse's neck. "What have I done?"

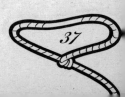

Scarlet whinnied in pain. Molly and Button watched from the fence. Tears were brimming in Sarah's eyes as she looked at her beloved horse, who was clearly in agony.

"What have I done?" she asked.

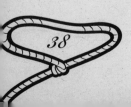

CHAPTER 7

Back in the stable, Sarah picked up an ice pack and held it to Scarlet's swollen ankle. Molly fed the mare hay out of a bucket.

"What did the vet say?" Molly asked, concerned.

"'Wait and see,'" Sarah replied. "It could be a sprain . . . or a whole lot worse."

Sarah covered her face with her hand, her voice cracking. "I can't believe I pushed her like that! What's wrong with me?" Sarah had

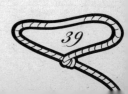

never felt worse. If she had just listened to Molly and gone inside with the others, none of this would have happened.

"You're the can-do kid, Sarah," Molly said, trying to be supportive. "You don't give up until you can do what you want to do."

"But she was exhausted!" Sarah cried. "Why didn't I see it?" Sarah took another look at Scarlet's leg. It was more than she could bear. Crying, she stood and hugged Scarlet's neck. "I'll never forgive myself," Sarah said, burying her head in Scarlet's neck. She let out a deep sob. Scarlet nuzzled Sarah's face, her pink tongue lapping the tears from her cheeks.

"See, she forgives you," Molly said softly. "Why can't you forgive yourself?" But it was useless.

"Because I should know better! I wanted to get the move down so badly that I wasn't paying a bit of attention to what she was trying to tell me!" Furious, Sarah pulled the dressage instructions from her pocket and

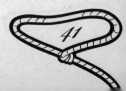

ripped them in two. She looked at Scarlet and hugged her neck again. "Scarlet wasn't cut out for this!"

"You don't ever have to do the lateral move step again, okay?" she told her horse. Scarlet turned sharply toward Sarah and let out a whinny. What was the point of all that practice if they were just going to give up now?

In the next few weeks Sarah visited Scarlet every day. She brought her carrots, combed her long black mane, and cleaned out her hooves. But, most important, she carefully iced and wrapped Scarlet's ankle, watching as the swelling slowly went down. Sarah applied salve and massaged Scarlet's leg.

"That feel good, girl?" she asked, as she stroked the Arabian mare's side.

Soon the swelling had gone down, and the vet came and went—this time, with bet-

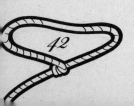

ter news. Scarlet was going to be okay. Sarah opened the stable door and led the horse outside. Molly and Alma watched as Scarlet stepped gingerly on her bad foot. She tossed her head back in the air and let out a whinny.

She was happy to be outside again.

"Look, guys! Scarlet's almost all better," Sarah said. "Her leg is a lot less swollen than last week." Alma watched Scarlet prance around, her tail whipping back and forth.

"She sure does seem happy," Molly said.

"How about we go on a trail ride in a couple of days?" Alma suggested. It had been a long time since all the girls had ridden together.

"Sounds good to me," Sarah said, smiling with relief. "What about you, Scarlet—what do you think?" she asked, stroking Scarlet's nose. Scarlet let out a long excited whinny.

"And I promise," Sarah added, "no more lateral step. Ever." With that, Scarlet jerked her head away from Sarah and trotted off to the stable.

As Scarlet walked back into her stall, Button turned to her, her mouth full of hay. It was

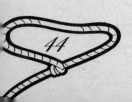

obvious something was troubling her friend.

"I thought your foot was getting better," Button said, puzzled.

"It is," Scarlet said with a sigh.

"Then why aren't you two practicing?" Button asked.

"She's giving up," Scarlet said, frustrated.

Just then, they heard Chili and Pepper in their stalls. They were high stepping around as mice dashed between their hooves.

"Shep, you said you were taking care of this!" Chili called to the shepherd dog. "Where's that lazy cat?"

Shep stood in the doorway, watching the scene. Angora was hopeless. You could bring a cat to the stable, but you couldn't make her hunt mice.

"She says she's not into doing favors," Shep replied.

"Not into it?" Chili said in disbelief. "How'd she like mice in *her* food?" Shep cocked his head to the side and smiled. That

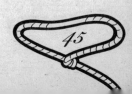

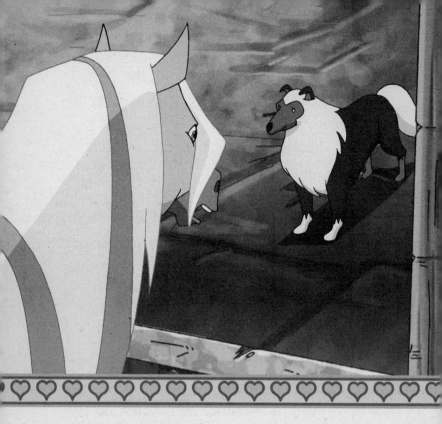

was just what he needed to hear—it gave him an idea. Maybe the situation wasn't so hopeless after all.

"Thanks, Chili," he said, as he walked lightly out of the stable. "You just gave me the solution to this problem."

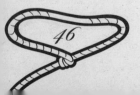

CHAPTER 8

Sarah picked up her peanut butter and jelly sandwich and took a huge bite. She smiled as she looked around the open field. This was the first good day she'd had in a long time. Scarlet's leg had healed, and she and Alma had just finished a long trail ride. Spread out on a blanket, they were eating the most perfect picnic lunch.

"Mmm, this is great," Sarah said, her mouth full of bread.

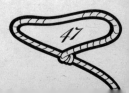

"So are you really giving up the lateral step?" Alma asked.

Sarah nodded. "I learned my lesson," she said, smoothing the checkered blanket. "I'm not pushing Scarlet to do something she hates."

A few yards away, Scarlet lifted her head and perked up her ears. Button looked over at her, sensing her annoyance.

"I don't hate lateral moves," Scarlet said,

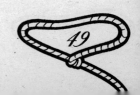

frustrated. "If she'd just learn to be patient and not rush it. All we need is more practice."

Just then, dark clouds rolled in, blocking out the sun. Thunder sounded in the distance.

"Oh, no!" Alma cried, looking up at the sky. "Not more rain."

"We'd better get back," Sarah said to Alma, as she put the remaining food back into the wicker basket.

Sarah and Alma made their way along the trail to Horseland. Another roll of thunder split the silence of the afternoon. From behind them, Sarah and Alma could hear a horse's nervous whinny. It was Chili. Chloe and Zoey were returning from their own trail ride, and Chili and Pepper joined Button and Scarlet on the wide trail.

"Hold on, Pepper," Zoey whispered in Pepper's ear. "It's just some puddles. We'll be

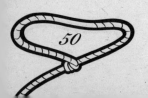

back soon." Zoey looked up at the long trail ahead of them and got an idea.

"We know a shortcut up ahead. There's a bridge," Zoey said. "Pepper is getting freaked out from all the rocks falling on the trail and all the slippery mud."

"Yeah," Chloe agreed. "Let's get home faster." Just then, lightning flashed in the sky again. Sarah and Alma glanced at each other. Alma shrugged.

"Fine with me," Sarah said as she galloped ahead. "Let's go!" Scarlet ran on four strong legs. Her injury was fully healed and she was enjoying the run.

"Lead the way," Alma cried. The storm continued to gather around them. Pepper then bounded ahead, pounding through a puddle to direct the others to the shortcut.

The girls approached an old wooden bridge, which spanned a river dotted with fallen boulders. The first span of the bridge connected to a narrow strip of rocky island in the center of the river. The second span of

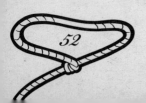

the bridge connected that island to the opposite shore. Chloe looked down at the bank.

"Whoa, that water looks high," she said, a little nervous.

Without hesitation, Sarah rode Scarlet onto the first part of the bridge. Alma followed Sarah, but Chloe and Zoey hesitated as they looked at the rickety bridge.

"I guess she forgot about 'taking it one hoof at a time,'" Zoey said. The dark skies continued to threaten the girls' safe return to Horseland. Chloe and Zoey cautiously started across the bridge, but then a wobbly plank of wood gave way under Pepper's hoof. The sisters screamed.

The bridge was collapsing beneath them! Chili and Pepper bucked and panicked as they lost their balance. Another board cracked and plummeted, dropping just a few inches above the raging river. Pepper reared up, terrified. The section of the bridge that connected to the island was still intact,

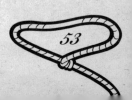

53

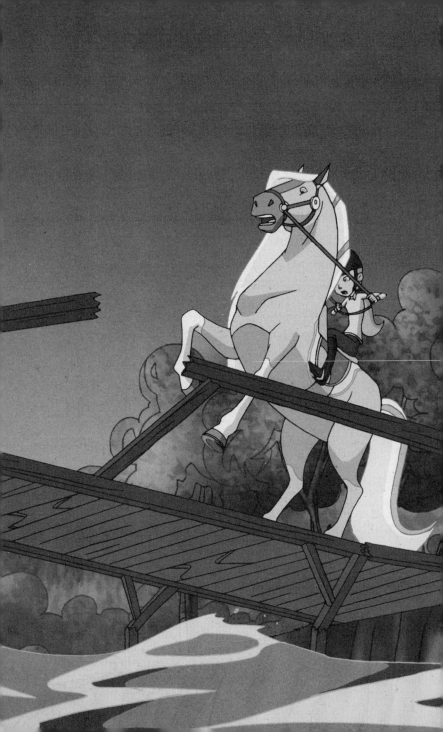

though, and as Sarah and Alma watched the scene, they knew what they had to do. Sarah dug her knees into Scarlet's side, urging her forward.

"Come on," she screamed to the girls. "Run for it!"

The girls spurred their horses forward onto the small island. The bridge fell apart behind them. Chloe and Chili pushed off the remaining planks and leaped onto solid land, just as the last wooden beam fell down into the water and rushed away.

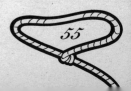

CHAPTER 9

Alma and Sarah stroked their horses' necks, trying to calm them. That was a close call. Chloe and Zoey had nearly been swept down the river with the broken bridge.

"Whoa," Chloe cried, "that bridge was going, going, gone."

Scarlet whinnied. The thought of losing her friends, plus being stuck on the island, was very upsetting. Sarah leaned forward, resting her head on Scarlet's neck.

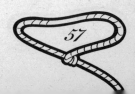

"Shhh, it's okay, girl," she said in a small voice.

Zoey, terrified, held tightly to Pepper's reins and began to shout, unable to form complete sentences.

"Whoa. We could have been, like—and then we would have been—and *whoa*." She wheeled Pepper around, spurring the horse toward the next span of the bridge on the other side of the island.

"That was too close," Chloe said.

"Let's get out of here!" Zoey agreed. And with that, Pepper galloped onto the second section of the bridge that spanned the other side of the river. But the old wooden planks creaked under her weight. The gray mare panicked and let out a loud whinny.

"This bridge is breaking, too!" Zoey cried.

"Back up!" Sarah yelled. Zoey pulled Pepper back onto the island just as the side rails of the bridge slowly collapsed into the river, leaving a very wobbly and dangerous

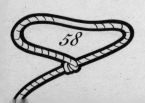

path to the shore. Zoey dismounted from Pepper onto shaky legs. Chloe ran to her sister and threw her arms around her.

"Zoey, you almost—" But Chloe stopped herself. It was too horrible a thought.

"I wish I had never even thought of this shortcut," said Zoey, frightened.

Boards were littered among the rocks at different angles. Alma and Sarah turned their horses in different directions, looking for another way off the island. Sarah led Scarlet down the steep bank, but Scarlet let out a frustrated grunt and backed away. The water was raging.

"Let me try," Alma said. The river roared around them, the bank just a few inches above the water. Alma walked Button into the water, but Button balked, backing out of the wild rapids. The river was just too deep, too wide, too fast.

Alma looked at Sarah, her face full of concern. "There's no way out of here," she said, hopeless. Thunder rumbled again. All

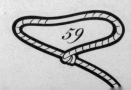

the horses moved nervously about, spooked by the loud sound. Heavy drops of rain began to fall. The girls pulled out their cell phones, but there was no signal.

"No service," Chloe said.

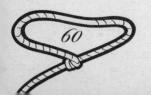

"Same here," Sarah added. Zoey slid her own cell phone back into her pocket, too.

"The others will notice we're missing," Zoey said, hoping that would happen *sooner* rather than later.

"They'll send somebody to rescue us," Alma added. Sarah watched as the rain pounded on the surface of the river. Upstream, a tree crashed over, brought down by the storm.

"The river's rising. We can't afford to wait," Sarah said. As the river water splashed up and over the edge of the narrow island, the girls knew she was right.

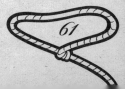

CHAPTER 10

Sarah slipped off Scarlet to examine what was left of the second bridge. Some of the planks had washed downstream, but the wide sections that were left created a precarious path almost all the way to the far shore. Sarah stepped onto the nearest plank, letting it absorb some of her weight. It was stable, but it probably wouldn't hold up under the weight of four horses and their riders. Watching from behind her, Scarlet let out

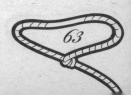

a curious neigh. Sarah shook her head, nervous.

"We can't do it, Scarlet," she said. "We'd have to do the lateral steps." Scarlet's leg had just healed—how could Sarah make her do dressage moves after all that had happened? This was too dangerous. But Scarlet pushed her nose into Sarah, making her look at her.

"You really want to try?" Sarah asked, still uncertain. Scarlet pawed the ground and tossed her head back. They were really going to do it. Sarah pulled herself up and into the saddle. Alma looked at her, shocked.

"You can't be serious," she said.

"Look at the planks. It's perfect for the lateral move," Sarah explained. Zoey raised her eyebrows.

"I thought you gave up on that," she said, acting confused.

"We can do it," Sarah said confidently, as she turned toward the bridge. For once,

Zoey and Chloe were speechless.

"Nice and slow, Sarah," Alma said encouragingly. "One hoof at a time."

Sarah turned Scarlet toward the first board, pulling on her left rein as she pressed her right leg into Scarlet's side. "Here we go, Scarlet," she whispered. "Nice and easy." Scarlet took her first step, then her next, moving laterally along the board, slowly but surely, each hoof placed carefully along the narrow plank. Alma pressed her hands deep into her pockets, barely able to watch. As Scarlet and Sarah reached the end of the first plank, Scarlet rested her hoof on the second plank. She put her full weight on the board, and it wobbled and then dropped suddenly into the water. Scarlet stumbled and nearly fell into the rushing river. Sarah braced herself in the saddle. Alma gasped.

"The bridge is buckling!" Zoey cried.

Scarlet reared back, and Sarah almost lost her grip on the reins. Sarah looked behind

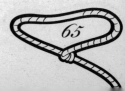

her at the section of the bridge they had successfully crossed. The shore was now several feet away. They had gone too far. There was no turning back.

CHAPTER 11

"**S**teady, girl," Sarah whispered into the hollow of Scarlet's ear. Scarlet took a few quick steps along the board and recovered her balance.

"Okay, girl," Sarah said, relieved. "Let's try the next one." Scarlet put her hoof down on the next plank, which rocked back and forth. She let out a frightened snort. Sarah looked up. They were in the middle of the river—a little more than halfway to the other shore. If only they could go just a little farther . . .

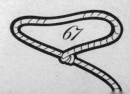

She stroked Scarlet's mane. "Take it slow. One step at a time . . . ," she said reassuringly. Scarlet waited until the board settled. Then she took the lateral step. Sarah couldn't help but smile. "That's it. One hoof at a time," she said softly.

Alma peered out from behind her hands, which were covering her eyes. She was happy to see Sarah and Scarlet stepping slowly but confidently. They were doing the lateral move perfectly to the end of the third plank! Scarlet checked her footing before putting her full weight on the fourth and final plank. Scarlet took another sideways step, smoothly heading down the plank. Sarah pulled at the reins and Scarlet made a small leap to the shore. They made it!

"Good girl, good girl!" Sarah cried, as she threw her arms around Scarlet's neck. "We did it!" Scarlet let out a happy whinny. Sarah pulled Scarlet to face the other girls and waved. Alma jumped up and down and let out a delighted shriek. She was so relieved.

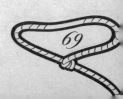

"Way to go!" she called. "You guys are awesome!"

Sarah smiled. "Don't go anywhere!" she yelled. "We'll be right back!"

The rain was coming down in sheets now, and Chloe and Zoey folded their arms across their chests, trying to keep warm.

"Where are we going to go?" Zoey asked, shivering. Sarah spun Scarlet around and set off into the woods.

"Come on, Scarlet!" she cried, and the horse broke into a fast gallop.

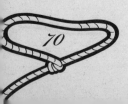

CHAPTER 12

Sirens blared as three rescue vehicles pulled up to the riverbank. The rescue workers stretched a portable metal bridge across the rushing water to the island. Sarah watched as Alma, Chloe, and Zoey led their horses over the bridge to land. They were soaking wet, but otherwise okay. Alma rushed toward Sarah, her arms outstretched. They hugged tightly. Sarah was so relieved to see that everyone was safe.

"Come on," Sarah said, comforting her

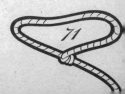

friends. "Let's get all of you warmed up." Sarah turned to leave, but Chloe stepped in front of her. She looked oddly nervous.

"Sarah—we—well, we want to thank you."

Zoey joined her sister. "And Scarlet, too," she added. Sarah's mouth dropped open. Was she imagining things?

"I guess it's not such a bad thing you did all that practicing," Chloe said, the slightest of smiles crossing her face. Then she pulled Sarah into a hug. As soon as Chloe let go, Zoey hugged her, too, their sopping-wet riding clothes making an odd squishing sound.

Sarah went over to Scarlet and rested her hand on the horse's cheek. She looked into the mare's soft blue eyes. "You did it, girl. You saved us," she said.

"No, Sarah," Alma said shaking her finger in the air, "you both did. Together." Scarlet neighed in agreement and nuzzled Sarah's cheek.

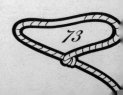

That evening, in the living room of the Horseland Ranch house, the girls drank cocoa and warmed themselves by the fire, happy to be safe . . . and dry. Zoey pulled the towel from her head and let her red hair lay flat against her face.

"I look like a wet turnip, don't I?" Zoey asked. Chloe smiled.

"More like a wet—brussel sprout," she said giggling. Zoey nudged Chloe in the side. Sarah barely noticed the girls. She was sitting cross-legged on the couch, a towel wrapped around her head. She was engrossed in a letter.

"What's that?" Alma asked, peeking over Sarah's shoulder.

"The tri-county dressage competition. With a special event—lateral moves. It's at the end of next month," Sarah said.

Chloe and Zoey exchanged an amused look.

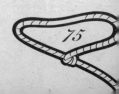

"I thought you were never *ever* doing lateral moves again," Chloe teased. But this time Chloe's words didn't bother Sarah.

"Me?" she asked, pretending she'd forgot. "Did I say that?"

In the stables, the horses were covered in blankets, their troughs filled with plenty of carrots. Pepper let out a wheezy snore. Button munched on some hay—suddenly, she stopped chewing. Something was different.

"Hear that?" Button asked the others.

"I don't hear anything," Calypso replied.

"I know," Button said. "The mice are gone!" Shep, who was lying on a bale of hay a few feet away, raised his head.

"I wondered when you would notice." He laughed, looking at the horses, their heads peeking out of each stall.

"How'd you do it, Shep?" Chili asked.

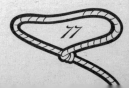

"Remember how you said you didn't like mice in your food?" Shep asked. The horses nodded. "Well, Teeny and I moved Angora's pillow to the feedbags. So she's going to have to chase those mice away before she can take another catnap." Shep and the horses listened as Angora's high-pitched screech filled the air.

"Outta here!" she screamed, as mice darted out of the barn. "Right now!"

CHAPTER 13

I n the arena, Will is still practicing his lassoing. He tosses the rope high in the air and lets it fall toward the post. The lasso just misses the post. Angora lounges in the arena, every now and then taking a bite from her food bowl. Shep sniffs it and coughs.

"Aw, Angora—what are you eating?" Angora licks her lips and smirks at Shep.

"Sardines—the most delectable breakfast on Earth."

"The stinkiest anyway," Shep replies. Will

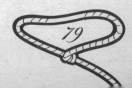

79

launches the lasso in the air again, and this time it falls to the ground, just inches from Angora.

"This kid never gives up," she says in disbelief. "Why can't he just accept the fact that he's never going to get it?" Teeny nods. She hates to agree with Angora, but the cat has a point.

"He *has* been at it for days and days now," Teeny says. Will focuses his eyes again on the fence post, concentrating as hard as he can. He swirls the rope above his head.

"It takes patience and perseverance to learn to lasso," Shep says, defending Will. "Sooner or later, he'll get it."

The lasso once again flies from Will's hands, soars to Angora's bowl of sardines, and this time ropes the bowl, yanking it off the bale of hay and away from the cat.

"Hey!" Angora cries, chasing the bowl of sardines.

Shep grins at Teeny. "What did I tell you?" he says. "He got it!"

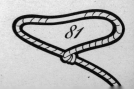

Meet the Riders
and Their Horses

Sarah Whitney is a natural when it comes to horses. Sarah's horse, **Scarlet**, is a black Arabian mare.

Alma Rodriguez is confident and hard-working. Alma's horse, **Button**, is a skewbald pinto mare.

Molly Washington has a great sense of humor and doesn't take anything seriously—except her riding. Molly's horse, **Calypso**, is a spotted Appaloosa mare.

Chloe Stilton is often forceful and very competitive, even with her sister, Zoey. Chloe's horse, **Chili**, is a gray Dutch Warmblood stallion.

Zoey Stilton

is Chloe's sister. She's also very competitive and spoiled. Zoey's horse, **Pepper**, is a gray Dutch Warmblood mare.

Bailey Handler

likes to take chances. His parents own Horseland Ranch. Bailey's horse, **Aztec**, is a Kiger mustang stallion.

Will Taggert is Bailey's cousin and has lived with the family since he was little. Because he's the oldest, Will is in charge when the adults aren't around. Will's horse, **Jimber**, is a palomino stallion.

Spotlight on Aztec

Breed: Kiger mustang

Physical Characteristics:

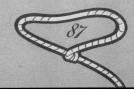 Tan or light brown/grayish coat with dark brown
or black mane

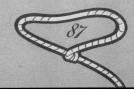 Dark coloring around the muzzle and ears

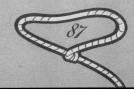 Legs that are usually darker than the body

- ♘ Zebralike stripes on the upper legs and shoulders
- ♘ A stripe running down the middle of the back into the tail (called the dorsal stripe)

Personality:
- ♘ Agile
- ♘ Intelligent
- ♘ Good stamina and sure-footedness
- ♘ Bold, courageous, and determined
- ♘ Gentle

Fun facts:
- ♘ The Kiger mustang is a descendant of the horses brought to America by Spanish conquistadors.
- ♘ Many of today's existing Kiger mustangs can be traced back to a single stallion named *Mesteno*, which means "stray" in Spanish.

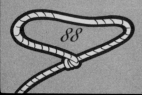

Bailey's
Dressage 101

Dressage (a French word meaning "training") is a method used to develop a horse's natural athletic ability and willingness to perform. It can help make the horse easier to ride. Dressage teaches horses to be agile, balanced, and cooperative. A horse trained in dressage can respond to a rider's cues by performing a requested movement while

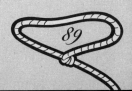

remaining relaxed. Because a skilled horse can make any dressage movement look graceful and effortless, dressage is sometimes called "horse ballet." Any breed can be trained in dressage, but thoroughbreds or warmbloods are preferred.

Dressage competitions are held at every level, and it is even an Olympic event.

- In competition, the riders guide their horses through a series of movements at the walk, trot, and canter, using mainly leg and seat signals.
- A good rider's signals are not visible to the spectators.
- The series of movements is performed by one rider and horse team at a time, in a marked rectangular arena.
- The movements are done in a specific order, and each movement in the exercise is judged and scored on a scale of 0 to 10; the horse and rider with the most points win.

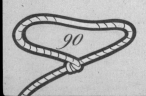

♘ Special dressage movements include the *passage*, *piaffe*, and *pirouette*.

- A passage is a rhythmic, elevated trot in which the horse slowly moves forward.
- A piaffe resembles a trot, but it is performed without any forward, backward, or sideward movement.
- A pirouette is a circle that the horse makes by pivoting its forelegs and one hind leg around the other hind leg.

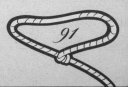

CHECK OUT THE NEXT ADVENTURE IN HORSELAND!

Based on the CBS Saturday morning animated show *Horseland*.

Everyone at Horseland Ranch knows that competing is a natural part of the horseback riding world. But only one of the kids can represent Horseland at the upcoming Nashville Nationals. They each work hard to become the best Western rider at the ranch, and friendly competition quickly turns to hurt feelings. Chloe is named Horseland's entry, but she soon realizes that winning back her friends may be even harder than winning the contest.

READ ABOUT ALL OF YOUR FAVORITE CHARACTERS AT HORSELAND RANCH:

HarperEntertainment
An Imprint of HarperCollins*Publishers*

WWW.HARPERCOLLINSCHILDRENS.COM